THIS BOOK
BELONGS
TO

For Olivia, thank you for always being my biggest inspiration. Keep being unapologetically you.

First paperback edition August 2023.
ISBN: 9798859215188

The ABSURD Ladybird

Written By
Sarah Crisp

Illustrated By
Lee Dixon

To Mae,

Remember, there is no one else quite like you!

Crisp

Humdrum Town was a boring place
where everyone had a frown on their face.

The flowers drooped, the birds wouldn't sing, and everyone wore the exact same thing.

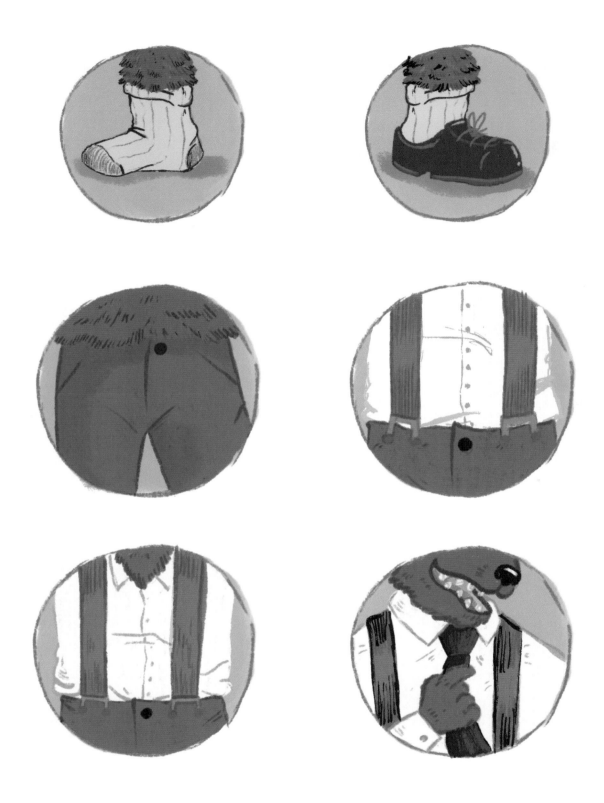

Socks that were beige, and shoes with laces,
pintuck trousers and a pair of braces. A tucked-in
shirt that was crisp and white,
with a long black tie, as dark as the night.

That was of course, except ladybird,
who liked to dress quite absurd.
Floral wellies with a dress that was red,
and a light pink bonnet worn on her head.

Ladybird was different to the rest
of town; she was bold and
cheerful and not one to frown.

She would dance and prance
through the street, smiling and waving
at the people she'd meet.

They'd return with a grunt and an almighty
moan, and tell ladybird in a stern tone.

*"Ladybird, ladybird can't you see, you dress
a little differently. You're not the same as
all of us, you flutter and flounce and make
a fuss. Humdrum Town is not for you,
now off you go."*

So away she flew.

She sighed a sigh that was full of
despair, not wanting friends to
scowl and stare. She packed her bags and
flew away - looking for a new place
to stay.

Up ahead, she saw a peculiar sight - a place
that was vibrant, dazzling, and bright.
She fluttered her wings down to
the ground and was delighted by what she
had found.

The flowers bloomed, and the birds loved to sing. Everyone was happy and smiling.

"Hello! Good morning!" they said cheerfully, as they skipped along, dressed differently.

She saw llamas in pyjamas that were
covered in spots, and goats in coats tied
with knots. There were giraffes
in scarves wrapped around their neck, and skunks
in trunks patterned in check.

"Goodness me!" exclaimed ladybird,
"Everyone is dressed quite absurd."
She twisted and twirled, watching
people pass by. Vibrant patterns and colours
catching her eye.

She saw pigs in wigs, curly and straight, and ants
in pants that had woken up late.
There were crows with bows tied on their
chests, and hares in flares with stripy vests.

Her stomach felt fuzzy and
full of delight,
as she marvelled at this place
so happy and bright.

"Everywhere I look, there's
new things to see,
I hope I find a
ladybird just like me."

She saw gazelles with bells tied on
their shoe, and geese in fleece
in shades of blue. There were frogs in clogs
with dancing feet, and crocs in frocks
with pleats so neat.

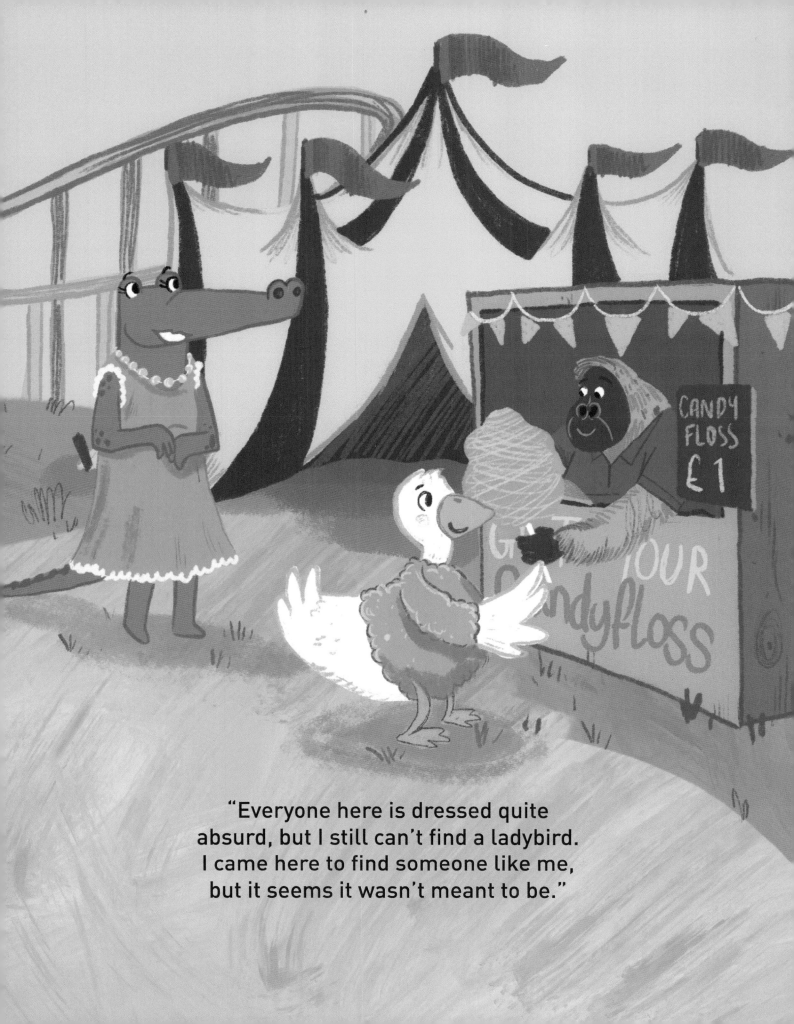

"Everyone here is dressed quite
absurd, but I still can't find a ladybird.
I came here to find someone like me,
but it seems it wasn't meant to be."

"There aren't any ladybirds with a dress
that's red, or a light pink bonnet worn
on their heads." Feeling full of sorrow
and sadness too, ladybird opened her wings,
and off she flew.

WOLLAP! BANG! She crashed with a thud and fell to the ground, landing in mud! "I'm sorry, excuse me," ladybird said, as she sat in the mud rubbing her head.

There before her stood a prestigious bee.
"Where are you off to in such a hurry?"
"I'm going back home to Humdrum Town,
where I'll grumble, groan and have a frown."

Her eyes welled up, feeling all alone,
and a teardrop fell as she let out a groan.
The bumblebee smiled and rubbed
her head, and in a soft voice,
he turned and said:

"Ladybird, ladybird can't you see; we all dress a little differently. We're not the same as anyone, but we laugh and dance and have lots of fun.

It doesn't matter what clothes you wear,
what matters is how you show you care.
To share a smile or say a kind word
makes you great, not absurd!

Being different is special, it doesn't mean
you're weak, you're awesome,
you're perfect,
and you are unique!

Keep singing and dancing to your
own special song,
and to those who say 'STOP', tell them they're
wrong.

You're brave, you're kind,
and thoughtful too, remember,
there is no one else quite like you."

Printed in Great Britain
by Amazon

27589478R00018